THE GUNFIGHTER IN WINTER

A Jack Cordell Western

R. Annan

Dedicated to

Anthony R. Annan, SGM, USA, Retired

1.

The three riders were well strung out when the snow began to thicken. The leader, big Chub Hurley, the Bar J ramrod, pulled his horse up short. The snow had been falling for the last two hours now, all but blotting out the trail to the line shack. Everywhere he looked he saw a thick blanket of cotton covering the earth. He tightened the collar of his mackinaw up around his beefy neck to keep out the cold as he waited for the other two to catch up. His breath came out in little white puffs that faded in the frigid Kansas air.

Jeb Frankel, Hurley's second-in-command, a tall, rangy cowboy, looked back at a slowly advancing rider.

"Come on, you old coot! Hurry it up or we'll leave you behind!"

The old coot, Nate Prescott, came slowly towards the other two. His small, thin frame shook from the cold. He pulled his hat down over his ears.

Hurley looked around just as a coyote howled off in the distance. Nate finally caught up.

"It don't make no sense us comin' all the way up here like this," old Nate whined through chattering teeth. "Couldn't it a waited until the thaw?"

"If Chub said it's time to check it out, then it's time to check it out," Frankel said. "So stop yer bitchin'."

"It coulda waited 'til April, couldn't it? That line shack ain't goin' nowhere, is it?"

"Aw shut the hell up, old man. I don't know why Chub didn't cut you lose a long time ago. You're as useless as tits on a toad!"

Chub Hurley turned a menacing eye on the other two. "If you two don't stop actin' like fools, I'll fire you both!" he growled. He spurred his horse on ahead. Frankel and Prescott fell in behind him, pulling up their collars to keep the snow off their necks.

In an hour they saw the line shack in a gully near a stream. They stopped again to carefully study the area, and then walked their mounts cautiously over to it. The big man slowly got down. He bent over and stared at the ground by the hitching post.

The coyote howled again, this time closer.

"Someone has been here, boys," Chub Hurley said. Then, "Looks like the tracks is headin' towards the stream. You two go take a look. I'll check out the shack."

Jeb and Nate nudged their horses around the back of the line shack to the stream. Chub pulled his gun and eased the door open and stepped slowly in. It was cold and dusty inside. The pinewood floor groaned under the big man's weight.

The Bar J ramrod stood looking around to make sure no one was there. Satisfied, he holstered his gun. As he did so, he noticed something shiny on the table. It was two double eagles. He studied them for a moment before picking them up. He put them in his coat pocket and waited.

Moments later Jeb and Nate came in stomping snow off their boots.

"They was down by the stream," Jeb said. "They watered their horses and left."

"You're wrong, Jeb," Nate said. "It were only but one rider. Any fool could see that."

"How do you know, old man? I say it was at least two or maybe three."

Old Nate shivered and sniffed.

Chub grunted. "Well, whoever it was stole a blanket and took some grub. And that's stealin' in my book!"

The old man sniffed then wiped his nose with the back of his hand. "Well, that weren't right, I reckon."

"They took a cut of salted venison, some hard tack, and a can of peaches, too," Chub said. He looked around for a moment. "Which way are the tracks a headin'?"

"West," Jeb said.

Nate said, "Maybe it was just some saddle bum what got lost. A drifter, maybe."

"Whatta you think, Chub?" Jeb asked.

The ramrod gave the question a moment's reflection. "It coulda been anybody. Maybe the Box N boys."

"Aw, yer makin' a big fuss outta nothin', Chub," Nate said. "It were just some cowboy a passin' through!"

"Yeah? What if it ain't? What if, like Chub says, it were some of those Box N riders?" Old Nate only shrugged in defeat.

"There's only one way to find out," Chub said. "And that's to go after 'em." With that, he went outside into the snow. The others followed.

The three Bar J men mounted up. With Chub Hurley in the lead, they started following the tracks. It had gotten noticeably colder and the Kansas wind picked up the powdery snow and tossed it in their faces. It was difficult seeing up ahead. The going was slow.

The tracks followed a worn trail that wound between dark cedars and past spruce-berry ground cover. It was easier to see here. They followed it up over a small rise and down into a bowl of dry prairie grass. The wind howled like a mourning coyote as it slid down off the surrounding hills, pushing sheets of snow ahead of it.

Suddenly the trail seemed to end. They stopped to tighten the collars of their coats and shake the snow off their chaps.

"What now?" Jeb asked.

Chub Hurley looked around, an uncertain look on his face. Moments later he pointed. "Over there!" he shouted against the wind. Jeb and Nate looked across the bowl to a stand of aspens that stood bare and dark like sentinels against the pristine snow. They saw an opening between the trees.

Without another word, the big Bar J ramrod spurred his horse on, kicking up billows of snow that went curling into the wind. Jeb fell in behind him. Nate sat watching for a few seconds then urged his horse on.

"Damn fools," he said.

Jeb looked back. "What did you say, you old fart?"

"I'm cold," Nate yelled. Jeb chuckled. He took delight in the old man's misery.

They finally came to the rim of the bowl and rode into the aspens.

It was like entering another world. The wind screamed and the trees swayed and groaned as if alive. The sound of a thousand harps could be heard playing in the higher reaches. Nate looked up and saw hundreds of black things clinging to the swaying branches. They were crows taking refuge from the storm. When they saw the men and horses they shot heavenward in a spurt of speed, heading into the winds aloft, out of sight.

The three horsemen came out of the stand of aspens and picked up the trail once more, following it across an open area where a stream cut through it. There were some Bar J cattle along the stream's edge. The prairie grass in the area had been chewed low.

"This is a long way out for our cattle to be, ain't it, Chub?" Jeb asked.

"Yeah, sure is."

"They're just drifters, is all," Nate said. "They'll come back in the spring with yearlings."

"Or else somebody drove them out here," Chub said, looking around.

The other two followed, making a visual sweep of the area. Suddenly Jeb pointed to a cluster of pines and boulders to their left. Smoke drifted up, contrasted against the whiteness of the snow.

"We got 'em, boys," Chub said grimly. "Let's go."

They went off at a fast trot towards the rocks. Soon they came into a u-shape enclave where the boulders formed a protective barrier from the elements.

They saw a lone figure huddled over a small fire where a pot of coffee boiled. The man had a wool blanket around his shoulders. When he stood up to greet them, they saw he was wearing a gun. He didn't look like a cowhand. He was dressed in a suit and wearing a hat, but there was something more to him. It was his eyes. They had an alertness, as if he was studying them.

"Howdy, strangers," the man said. He waved his free hand. "Come on in!"

The Bar J men dismounted and came up to warm themselves by the fire. "Whatta you doin' here," Chub Hurley said coldly.

"Waiting for the storm to blow over."

"Where you headin'?" Nate asked.

"Nowhere in particular, friend," the stranger replied.

"Oh, a saddle bum, huh?" Jeb sneered.

The stranger only shrugged. "I'd offer you some coffee but I only have this one cup."

"Yeah, I know. You stole that and the coffee from the line shack a ways back," Chub sneered.

"I left two double eagles," the stranger said. "Didn't you see them?"

Chub turned to Jeb. "Did you see any double eagles, pard?"

"There weren't none that I know of," Jeb said with a scowl.

The stranger gave Chub a dubious look.

"You got any more of them double eagles, stranger?" Chub asked.

"Ah, no. They were my last two, friend," the man said.

Chub chuckled. "So you left your last two double eagles in a line shack, huh?" The stranger only shrugged.

Suddenly the snow started to thicken, dropping in on them in heavy sheets. The little fire sputtered and crackled. There was an eerie silence except for the voice of the wind.

"We don't take kindly to stealin' around here, mister," Chub said. He drew his gun and pointed it at the stranger.

"Get his gun, old man!"

"Now, wait a minute, boss," old Nate cried. "Maybe he did leave that money, like he said. An' somebody came along an' got it."

"Shut up and get his gun, you old fart!" Chub roared. Snow was now billowing into the hollow, making it hard to see.

"It's range hospitality to offer strangers grub an' shelter, ain't it?" Nate whined.

"You dumb, old goat!" Chub growled. "I always did think you were a little crazy." Then, "Get his gun or I'll blast you, you old son of a bitch! I'm boss here and you'll do as I tell ya'!"

"Relax," the stranger said. He slowly unbuckled his gun belt and dropped it. He kicked it over towards Jeb who picked it up and looped it over the saddle horn of his horse.

Nate began to whine and tremble.

"Christ!" Jeb Frankel said. "The old bastard is havin' one of his cryin' fits agin!"

"I told Mr. Jarvis he wasn't any good," Chub sneered. Then, "Get the hombre's horse."

Jeb grabbed the halter of the stranger's horse and led it over to his own mount and tied its reins to his saddle strap. The stranger watched, staring hard.

"What's your handles, friends?" the stranger asked.

"Why?" Chub asked.

"In case I come looking for you."

"You won't," Chub said coolly.

"Why not?"

"Because you'll be dead!"

Chub fired off a shot and the stranger fell backwards into the snow. The sound of the shot roared against the rocks. The horses whinnied and bucked backwards, rearing up, trying to break away.

"Grab 'em!" Chub yelled. He lunged at the reins of his horse.

Jeb managed to get hold of his own horse's halter. It took a few moments to settle all of them down. Chub and Jeb mounted up, but the old man slid down on his knees in the snow. He commenced to babbling some sort of hysterical gibberish, almost as if praying in a strange tongue.

Jeb shouted down at him. "Get on yer horse, old man!"

"Leave 'im," Chub roared. "We got no time fer his foolishness!"

"Leave 'im?" Jeb asked uncertainly.

Chub Hurley nodded. "Leave 'im!" He spurred his mount and rode off into the shroud of snow. Moments later Jeb caught up with him.

"He'll die out there, Chub," Jeb said.

"Then he won't be able to spread no stories."

"Yeah, right!" Jeb chuckled. "Let the old fool die. It was his choice, right?" Then, "Whatta we tell them back at the Bar J?"

"Tell 'em the old man just drifted off someplace. We turned around and he was gone."

"Yeah, that'll work. We'll spend the night at the line shack. When we get back to the Bar J we'll say when we woke up he was gone. Maybe the wolves got him and carried him off when he went out to take a crap."

They rode on quiet for a while until Jeb broke the silence. "Did you get a good shot at that hombre? Maybe he ain't dead."

"If my bullet didn't kill him, the cold will. Him and the old man will both be stiff as a board by morning."

"Yeah, I suppose so," Jeb replied. Then, suddenly, "His gun belt! It's gone! It must have come off when the horses bucked."

"Forget it. It's buried under the snow, by now."

They rode on for a few more miles when the stranger's horse pulled loose and ran off. Chub fired three shots at it as it disappeared into the mist of snow.

"I think you hit it," Jeb said.

Chub Hurley put his gun away. "Maybe."

They rode on.

2.

It took a while for the old man to realize just what had happened. He pulled himself together then walked over to stare down at the stranger's body. He bent down close to look. He heard breathing.

"You dead, mister?"

"Nope," the stranger groaned, "but my head hurts like hell!"

The man sat up. He had a bloody crease along his right temple, just above his ear. "Where's my hat, friend?"

Old Nate scrambled around. Found the strangers hat and gave it to him. By then the man was pressing his bandana against his head wound.

"Your gun, it's over there in the snow. I'll get it," Nate said.

"Thanks." The stranger watched Nate fish around in the snow. In a few seconds he found the gun belt and handed it over. The stranger wiped it clean and buckled it on.

"Real nice friends you got," the stranger said.

"The big bear, the one what shot you, is named Chub Hurley. He's the ramrod for the Bar J spread." The old man waited a moment to see if the stranger was impressed. He didn't seem to be. "The Bar J is owned by Mr. Jarvis. He's sort of king around these parts. The Bar J is the biggest spread in the valley." The stranger only nodded.

The man threw some dried prairie grass and pine needles on the dying fire. It sprang to life. The snow had slacked off.

For a moment the stranger and the old man stared at each other. The stranger saw a weather worn, skinny, dried-up old cowpoke at the end of his rope, lucky to get a job anywhere. The old man saw a thirty-something drifter who was self-confident, sure of himself, and ruggedly handsome enough to attract the ladies.

"You fast with that Colt, mister?" old Nate asked.

"Maybe. Why?"

"Well, you best be fast around here. If you ever run into Chub or his partner, Jeb, they'll have plenty of backup with them."

The stranger smiled.

"How about you? You fast with a gun?"

"I was once. Real fast." The old man sniffed. "They use to call me, Kid Prescott."

"Where you from, old timer?"

"I was born in Cheyenne, Wyoming."

"Then maybe I should call you, Cheyenne. How's that suit you?"

"That suits me just fine. What about you?"

"I'm from down around the Brazos River."

"Then I'll call you Brazos, if you don't mind, stranger. I kin remember that easier."

They both laughed and shook hands. The stranger groaned. He patted his wound with his bandana again.

"Whatta you gonna do about a horse?" Nate asked.

"They can't hold him. He knows where I am."

"Sounds like a smart horse," Nate said. "Where'd you find him?"

"I won him in a poker game," the stranger said. "His owner refused to give him up and drew on me. He was real fast."

"But not fast enough, it looks like."

"No, not fast enough."

They made small talk and shared a hot cup of coffee. It grew colder toward dark so they unsaddled Nate's horse and got him to lay down by the fire. They put some warm rocks between themselves and got under the blanket close to the horse. With their hats and coats on, and keeping the fire burning, they managed to get through the night without freezing to death.

Sometime during the night the stranger's horse came back.

Just before dawn then got up to melt snow for coffee and eat some jerky and hardtack. By sun up they were ready to re-saddle and go their separate ways.

"Well," old Nate said. "I guess this is where we part company, Brazos. Which way you a headin'?"

"West, I reckon...towards Montana, Cheyenne."

The old man liked being called Cheyenne. "Thets a long ways off, Brazos."

"Sure is, Cheyenne."

"You want some company, Brazos?"

The stranger and old Nate both knew he was finished at the Bar J. Knowing what he knew, Chub or Jeb would kill him on sight to keep him from telling.

"Yeah," the stranger said. "I really would like some company, partner."

The old man's face lit up. "Well, partner, let's get ta goin'."

They mounted and pointed their horses west just as the snow started falling heavy again. It seemed to get colder as the wind kicked up. The sky above hung low with grey clouds.

A few miles on, Nate said, "Do you like turnip and venison stew, Brazos?"

"I sure do. Why?"

"Well, if we head straight west we'll be passing through the Circle M spread. I hear widow McCloud keeps a big pot of turnip venison stew on the stove day and night, during the winter," Nate said. "Her kitchen is open to one and all. Cow boys and drifters alike. She's real hospitable."

"A widow, you say?"

"Yep. Young and purty and tough, she is, and the best cook this side of Chicago. Her apple and rhubarb tarts will just kill you! And her dirt cellar is full of preserves of all kinds."

"You're kidding."

"Nope! Honest injin! On my honor, partner, I swear I'm telling it true!"

The stranger chuckled. "You seem to know a lot about her."

"Well, shucks, everybody in the valley knows of widow McCloud's hospitality." Then, "Stop or no stop? Which is it gonna be?"

"We'll stop," the stranger said with a grin and a chuckle. "You got my mouth watering already, friend."

3

All the ranchers in Caldwell Springs Valley had a buckboard or two. But not Tern Jarvis. Instead of a buckboard, Tern "King" Jarvis, owner of the Bar J Ranch, had a two-wheeled cab that he imported from London. It had a covered top, comfortable, stuffed seat cushions, and protective doors on the side. The driver sat up high in the back with a long whip, and had a clear view of things ahead. During nasty weather he wore a rain slicker, helmet, and goggles. Tern Jarvis's cab was not only a thing of comfort, it was also a status symbol.

Jarvis liked English things and sometimes faked an English accent to impress people, especially when talking to his friends at the Cattlemen's Association in Caldwell Springs, a small cattle-shipping depot alongside the Santa Fe Railroad in central Kansas. He often spoke glowingly about his ancestors, falsely saying they came over to Jamestown in the early settlement days.

While Chub Hurley and Jeb Franklin were leaving old Nate Prescott out in the wilds and heading for an overnight stay at the Bar J line shack, Tern Jarvis was paying his weekly visit to the Cattlemen's Association Building where he would boast of his receipts and thriving stock portfolio gains.

As for Jarvis's wife, the poor woman had been thrown from a horse that she had whipped once too often and too harshly. It was an awful fall and broke her back. Of course, Jarvis made sure Bernice got the best of attention, and was attended by doctors, nurses, and servants. She was, however, condemned to life in a wheel chair.

The Jarvis ranch house was Bernice Jarvis's shining glory. Her husband bought the ranch from the bank on foreclosure when the owner was down on his luck and missed several payments. She rebuilt the original house to her specifications. It was two stories high, with six bedrooms, a huge dining room and kitchen, and rooms for three servants and two cooks. Her private stables were the envy of the valley.

Originally the ranch had been a small one. Over time, Tern worked with the banker, Seth Porter, to buy up all the ranches next to the Bar J. The Bar J was now the largest ranch in the area, and growing. It covered well over five hundred square miles, with over fifty thousand head of cattle. The only drawback was there wasn't quite enough water for that much stock. There was water, but not enough for such a large inventory. Water in the Caldwell Springs Valley was at a premium. Without more water, Jarvis could not expand. He wouldn't be satisfied until he owned every ranch in the valley.

So when Tern "King" Jarvis walked into the Cattlemen's Association Building, the other ranchers took notice. Some admired him, some feared him, but many both hated and feared him. They had seen how ruthless he could be, how he destroyed their friends. He could, and would, break anyone who dared to stand in his path.

As soon as Jarvis came up to the bar, the bartender was already mixing his rye and bitters on the rocks, stirred but not shaken. He took a sip and turned to rancher Ed Brown who was having a beer. They made small talk for a few moments, and Ed made an excuse to leave.

"Well, Ed," Jarvis said, "anytime you want to sell that little spread of yours, all I ask for is first refusal. Will you allow me that, Ed?"

"Oh, sure, Mr. Jarvis," Ed said. "Sure."

"Good. I'll hold you to that, Ed," Jarvis said. Brown owned the Flying B, a spread Jarvis had wanted for a long time now.

Ed Brown left. Jarvis finished his drink and walked across the room to join a small group of ranch owners. As he came near he thought he heard one of them mention Jan McCloud's name. She owned a small ranch, the Circle M, on the west edge of the Bar J.

"Did I hear someone mention the good widow McCloud's name, gentlemen?"

Rancher Cal Nelson, owner of the Box N, spoke up. "Oh, hello, Mr. Jarvis. I was just telling Al here it looks like the Circle M is about to fold." Al was Al Gordon, owner of the Oval G Ranch.

Tern Jarvis took out a gold cigar case and removed a Havana Bravura. He clipped the end with his cigar tool and poked a hole in its center. He stuck it slowly into his mouth, then took a matching gold matchbox from his vest pocket and lit the cigar. The ranchers watched the ritual with blank stares. Jarvis blew a cloud of sweet scented smoke above their heads.

"Cigar, gentlemen?" Jarvis offered.

"No thanks."

Al Gordon chuckled. He rolled a cigarette from a pouch of tobacco that he kept in his shirt pocket. When he was finished he lit a match on the heel of his boot and lit the cigarette. He blew smoke over Jarvis's head and smiled.

"Please excuse me, men," Gordon said. "I have to see a man about a horse." He smiled and walked away.

"So, Cal, what's this about the Circle M spread?" Jarvis asked.

"Widow McCloud has missed two bank payments on a loan her husband took out last year," Cal Nelson said.

"Oh?" Jarvis said, pretending to care. "Too bad. Are you sure about that?"

"Yep. I got it straight from the banker himself, last week, Tern."

For a moment Tern Jarvis's eyes glared hot. He didn't like these small-minded people calling him by his first name. He would make Nelson pay for that someday.

"So, Seth Porter told this to you, did he?" Jarvis asked just to verify the fact.

"Naw, it was Rolly Snead," Cal Nelson said. Rolly Snead was the man who served the eviction notices on those who missed four payments on their mortgages or loans. "He said old Seth Porter was tryin' ta figure a way to help the widow out with the board of trustees."

"Oh? Well, how thoughtful of old Seth," Jarvis said.

Suddenly Cal Nelson looked at his pocket watch. He forced a smile. "Well, gotta go pick up some sundries for the misses, Tern. See ya later." He walked off, leaving Jarvis alone.

Jarvis looked around the room, searching for a friendly face. He finally saw Lou Reynolds standing alone over in a far corner. He walked casually in his direction, blowing smoke as he went.

When he reached Lou he said, "I say, Lou, good to see you, old chap!" Jarvis went into his Englishman mode. Lou, whose Running R spread was larger than the others, smiled weakly, as if he felt cornered.

"Oh, hello, Jarvis," Reynolds said, holding a glass of whiskey in one hand and a cigarette in the other. He was unsteady on his feet, and his voice was thick from too much drink.

"How is the little lady, Lou?" Jarvis asked.

"Fine," the rancher answered. "Expecting another addition to the tribe."

"Oh? Congratulations, old boy. How many is that, now?" Jarvis asked.

"Eight, unless its twins."

"Heavens forbid!" Jarvis pretended concern. He watched Reynolds take another drink. His cigarette was so short it was about to burn his fingers.

"How many in your tribe?" Reynolds asked. He suddenly realized he had blundered. Jarvis had no children due to his wife's condition. "Sorry, I'm a little drunk."

Reynolds walked away, leaving the other man with an angry scowl on his face. Jarvis went to the bar and ordered another drink. He drank it quickly and ordered another. After finishing that he went downstairs to where he found his driver waiting in a foyer chair. In a few moments he was back in his cab and heading for the Majestic Hotel on the far side of town.

The lobby was dark and empty except for a bellhop dozing in a chair. Jarvis's driver sat down on a chaise while

Jarvis went up to the desk. The desk clerk came out from the back office and without a word, gave Jarvis a key to room twenty. The rancher went upstairs to the room without signing the register.

The desk clerk woke the bellhop and whispered something to him. He nodded and hurried off out into the night. A half hour later he returned with a female dressed in a hooded robe that covered her face. She went straight up to room twenty and entered without knocking.

4.

"We're being watched," Nate said. "Act casual like."

The stranger and the old man were well into the Circle M spread when three armed men came riding up to them with rifles drawn. The leader looked at old Nate and chuckled. They put their rifles away.

"Well, well," the leader, Tim Gary, the Circle M ramrod, said. "Looky here fellahs, if it ain't old Nate of the Bar J!" Then, "You're way off the reservation, ain't ya, old timer? How's things at the Bar J these days?"

"I ain't with the Bar J anymore, Gary."

"No? So, whatta ya doin' on Circle M land Nate?"

"My pard and me is headin' fer Montana."

"Well, then, just keep on a goin', you ain't there yet!" The other two cowboys laughed.

"I gotta tell the widow something, first," Nate said. "Something she should hear."

"So you say, old man," Gary smirked.

The other two young Circle M men, Henry Fuller and Pete Knowles, came close to the stranger, boxing him in.

"What's yer handle, mister," Fuller said with a touch of authority in his voice. The stranger nudged his horse back to put some space between them.

"Don't crowd me, sonny-boy," the stranger said flatly. He stared at Fuller. "You're breath smells like cow shit."

"Why you ---" Fuller started to say, but Nate cut him off.

"He's called Brazos," Nate said. "He's a Texan."

Fuller chuckled and stared back at the stranger.

"They call you Brazos, huh?" Fuller looked around at Pete Knowles and Tim Gary. "Sounds kind of phony, if ya ask me." Then, to the stranger, "You look more like a two-bit four-flusher."

The stranger smiled over at Tim Gary. "You the ramrod here?"

"That's right. What about it?"

"Then you'd better teach the little boy here some manners or I'll have to spank him."

The kid looked at the stranger and smirked.

Tim Gary chuckled. "That little boy is the fastest draw you'll ever see, mister, so I'd be careful, if I was you!"

"He's a snot-nosed kid and he's gonna get hurt," the stranger said calmly.

Young Henry Fuller sneered and spit in the snow near the stranger's horse, knowing he had the other two Circle M men on his side. With a false sense of bravado he pulled his horse back, putting more space between him and the stranger then stopped and let his arm hand hang down near his Colt.

"You wanna talk or you wanna draw?" Fuller said, smiling confidently.

"And if I don't, then what?" the stranger asked.

"Well then I guess I'll just shoot yer ears off."

"Make your move, sonny," the stranger said.

Henry Fuller went for his Colt. He heard a gun blast one time, but it wasn't his. The stranger's gun was out and pointing at him, white smoke coming from the barrel and drifting upward in the cold air.

Fuller realized that blood was running down his neck. He reached up to feel his left ear lobe, to where it was nicked. It burned hotly. Another shot came and this time he felt a burning across his left temple. He swayed in the saddle and would have fallen had not Pete Knowles grabbed him. The earth seemed to spin around him. Suddenly Fuller threw up on his friend, Knowles, but he somehow did manage to get his Colt back in its holster.

Tim Gary looked closer at the stranger, trying to figure him out. He couldn't, so he turned to the old man. "You say you got something to tell Mrs. McCloud, old man?"

"Yep, I do," Nate said, as if getting married.

"Let's go then," Gary said. Then, "Pete? You need any help with Fuller?"

"I'm okay," Fuller said sullenly. He'd had the wind knocked out of his sails. He looked over at the stranger. "I'm sorry, mister."

"It's okay. We all make mistakes, Mr. Fuller."

They all fell in behind Tim Gary. As they went along, the stranger noticed how few cattle there were. He nudged his horse up alongside Gary's.

"Where's all your stock?"

"A lot were sold to keep the ranch going," Gary said. "And a lot were stolen."

"Any ideas who?"

"Nope." They rode on in silence for a while. "Ah, you're fast. Very fast. I'm glad you didn't hurt the kid. I need him."

"He was in a bad need of an attitude adjustment, is all. He'll be just fine."

Gary chuckled. "And he's a lot smarter, now, too. I hope he learned his lesson."

"Me, too. I'd hate to do it all over again."

They rode past some more small clusters of Circle M cattle digging under the snow. "What's the count?" the stranger asked.

"It used to be nearly seven…eight thousand. It's more like maybe four or five, now."

"It looks like somebody is sending the Circle M a clear message."

"What message is that?"

"Sell or else."

"Or else what?"

"Or else I'll whittle you down to zero and see how you like that."

"Yeah, that sounds like what's goin' on."

It was late afternoon when they rode into the yard of the Circle M's ranch house. Jan McCloud must have heard them coming because she was already on the porch to greet them. With her were her twelve-year old twins, Alice and Alex. They watched the cowboys dismount.

The stranger noticed the twins were towheads while Jan was auburn. She was young for a widow, about his age, maybe in her mid-thirties. She wore men's overalls, a man's shirt and hat, and boots. She was not frail by any means, and her face was both attractive and weathered.

"What happened, Mr. Fuller?" Jan McCloud asked, noticing the bloody bandana the young man held to his ear.

"His luck ran out ma'am," Tim Gary said.

Jan nodded. "It happens to the best of us. Mr. Knowles, please bring Mr. Fuller into the kitchen so I can attend to his ear."

Henry Fuller and Pete Knowles went up the porch steps into the house. The twins followed them in. Jan Mc Cloud looked down at the old man, and then at the stranger. He avoided her eyes, looking down at the snow. She turned back to the old man.

"Mr. Prescott! What brings you here on such a dreary cold day, you yourself looking a mite dreary?" As she spoke, the wind picked up a sheet of snow and sent it flying across the yard towards the bunkhouse. Crows cawed in the nearby bare cottonwoods.

"Could I have a word with you ma'am?" Nate asked in a shivery voice.

"Surely, Mr. Prescott," Jan said. "Come in!"

She motioned with one hand for them all to come up onto the porch. Following her into the house, they went to the kitchen to join Fuller and Knowles at the table. She got a medical kit from the cupboard and started attending to Fuller's ear and temple. He winced at the iodine.

The twins ran upstairs to play.

"Introduce me to your friend, Mr. Prescott?" she said without turning.

"Yes, ma'am. He's called Brazos," the old man said with pride. "And I'm now called Cheyenne!"

Jan McCloud glanced at Tim Gary and winked, as if to question the old man's sanity. She finished up with the ear and put the medical box away.

She faced Nate Prescott. "Alright, Mr. Prescott, what is it you want to tell me."

"If yer interested in knowin', I know for a fact who's rustlin' yer brand."

"The Circle Diamond boys? The Flying Z?"

"Not even close, ma'am," Nate said. "No, it were Chub Hurley and Jeb Frankel."

Jan McCloud was silent for a moment. She stared hard at the old man, as if in doubt.

"Do you have proof of that accusation, Mr. Prescott?"

"Yer proof is sittin' right here, Mrs. McCloud," Nate said, pointing a finger at himself. "I was in on it myself, a few times. Not every time, but quite a few times."

Jan McCloud let that information sink in a moment. "Is Mr. Jarvis aware of this?"

"That I can't say for sure, ma'am. But I kind of suspect he might be."

"But why? Mr. Jarvis has ten times as much stock as the Circle M, and for that matter all the ranches in the Valley. I don't think he'd chance being accused of stealing cattle. His reputation would be ruined here.

For a moment the old man looked confused.

Jan McCloud smiled and patted old Nate's arm. "You look awfully tired, Mr. Prescott. Would you like to spend the night here, in the bunkhouse? You and your friend?"

"Water," Nate said.

"You need some water?"

"No, Jarvis does."

The stranger spoke up. "I think Cheyenne means that Jarvis needs the Circle M water. He has too much stock and they're dying for lack of it. He's in a bind."

For the first time Jan McCloud really noticed the stranger. She looked him up and down and sideways. Without looking away, she said, "Mr. Gary, what happened to Mr. Fuller's ear and head?"

"Brazos shot him."

"And why did Mr. Brazos shoot Mr. Fuller in the ear and head?"

"Ah, to be fair, the kid drew on him," Tim Gary said. "It was all fair and open, ma'am."

Jan nodded then got some cups from the cupboard. She got a big pot from the stove and poured everyone a steaming hot cup of coffee, including herself.

She looked at the stranger. "So, what's your real name, Brazos?"

The stranger shrugged. "Like Cheyenne said, Brazos."

"Are you on the dodge?"

"To be honest, yes, ma'am."

"From the law?"

"Ah no, not the law."

"But you are running?"

The old man cut in. "We're headin' for Montana!"

"They don't have your picture on the Post Office wall, do they Mr. Brazos?"

"Not that I'm aware of, ma'am," the stranger said.

Jan McCloud chuckled. "Well, you're not a politician on the run, that's for sure!"

"I wouldn't swear to that ma'am," the stranger said. They all laughed.

The stranger suddenly became aware of a certain aroma. He looked over at the stove and saw the big pot of stew that the old man had bragged about. Jan McCloud noticed. She went to the cupboard again and got enough bowls to go around. "Mr. Knowles, go get the boys up from the bunkhouse."

Hours later, after finishing their meal and the kitchen was back in order, Tim Gary, Nate, and the stranger sat and talked with their host.

"How long have you been a widow, if I may ask?" the stranger said.

"Six months now, since he was shot in the back on the way home from the Cattlemen's Association meeting."

"Anybody doing anything about it?"

"Marshal Sledge says he's looking into it, but I don't expect much from him," Jan replied.

"Oh? Why not?"

"He didn't like George all that much. My husband was very outspoken. He called a spade a spade." The stranger nodded. Jan went on. "He suspected that the Marshal knew who was stealing our stock, and told him so to his face."

"You think the Marshal is in with Jarvis?"

"George did. Maybe he's right. I don't know."

They were quiet for a while. Finally the stranger said, "Well, I guess I'll take you up on that offer and stay the night in your bunk house, that is if the offer still stands, ma'am, and there's room."

Jan McCloud chuckled. "Room, sir? We used to bunk fifteen to twenty. Now we're down to seven. There's room a plenty, Mr. Brazos."

All the men got up and left. On the way to the nearby bunkhouse, Gary said, "We could use an extra gun, mister. I got a feeling it's gonna get too hot around here for just me and the kid to handle."

The stranger shrugged. "I'm not in that line of work, my friend."

"Okay, but just sleep on it, won't ya?"

"Sure, I'll do that, but don't expect me to change my mind any."

It started to snow real hard and the wind blew it in a big drift against one side of the bunkhouse. It was getting dark and cold.

5.

The Circle M cowboys got up just before daylight and ate at the bunkhouse. Before he left, Tim Gary told the stranger and the old man that Mrs. McCloud wanted them to have breakfast before they left for Montana. The smell of coffee, bacon, eggs, and sourdough biscuits drifted down from the kitchen.

When they got there the twins were just finishing up eating. Jan told Nate and the stranger to sit as she worked up two batches of food for them. An hour later they were stuffed to the gills. Jan sat across from them while they drank a third cup of coffee. The twins were putting a puzzle together in the dining room.

"I suppose Tim Gary talked to you two about staying on?" They nodded.

"To be truthful, ma'am, I'm no cowhand? I do better at cards," the stranger said. "Not that I can't wrangle a steer. It's well, I just can't see it as a living."

"What you really mean is that you don't want somebody else's troubles."

"Ah, well…" The stranger left it at that.

"It's an open offer, if you change your mind, Mr. Brazos."

"Ah, ma'am," the stranger said. "Just as a word of caution you should have a cowboy or two staying back here, just in case. You get my drift?"

"I can handle a shotgun pretty well, Mr. Brazos, thank you," Jan said stiffly.

"No offense, ma'am," the stranger said. He and Nate stood up. "Thank you for your wonderful hospitality, ma'am."

"Thank you, Mrs. McCloud," the old man said. "I'm sorry about all your troubles."

"I believe you are, Mr. Prescott," Jan said with a smile. They shook her hand and went down to the bunkhouse to get their saddles and saddlebags.

"We could stay here until the snow melts," Nate said wistfully. "Then move on to Montana."

"She'd get her hooks into you, and you'd want to stay on forever," the stranger said.

"I saw the way you looked at each other."

"It didn't mean anything. We were just looking each other over, is all. It didn't mean anything."

"Sure," the old man chuckled. "If you say so." He chuckled some more.

"What's so funny?"

"Yer afraid of her, that's what! She got to you, didn't she? Right from the first, yesterday. I saw it then."

"You're crazy, old man."

"Sure I am. Crazy as a loon."

Suddenly they heard the distant pounding of horses. It got louder and louder by the second, stopping only when it reached the fence in front of the ranch house. Nate and the stranger went to a window and stared up towards the fence gate. The old man stiffened.

"It's Chub Hurley!" the old man groaned, his voice cracking. "And he's got four others with him! Makes five altogether!"

"Yeah, and one of them is his pal, Jeb," the stranger said. He buckled on his gun belt and check the cylinder of his Colt and put it back in its holster. He and Nate continued to watch as Chub Hurley yelled at the house.

Finally Mrs. McCloud came out on the front porch by herself. She stood there proud and fearless, with the wind blowing in her hair.

"Good morning, ma'am," Chub Hurley yelled against the wind.

"What can I do for you, Mr. Hurley," Mrs. McCloud said loudly.

"Mr. Jarvis says he's prepared to give you whatever you want for the Circle M, Mrs. McCloud. Just name your price, ma'am, and it's yours. Now, that's fair, ain't it?"

"Tell Mr. Jarvis I appreciate his offer, sir, but I'm not inclined to sell the Circle M. At least not at this time."

"Ah, when would that time be, ma'am?"

"Perhaps never, Mr. Hurley," Jan said.

"Ma'am, if you don't mind my saying, you're in deep trouble at the bank," Hurley said. "You're gonna have to sell. You can't hang on much longer."

"Well, that's my problem, isn't it, Mr. Hurley? And it's no worry of yours, is it?"

The big man shifted in his saddle, his face taking on a stern, irritated look. He looked over at Jeb Frankel and nodded. Frankel nudged his horse into the yard and looked around. He saw a rooster clawing at the dirt beneath the snow and drew his gun. He shot the rooster. A dozen hens nearby squawked and leaped about, trying to escape. The Bar J man fired until his gun was empty and quickly reloaded. Feathers went flying in the wind. There were dead chickens and blood everywhere, in the snow.

Jeb Frankel holstered his gun and waited for further instructions from his boss. Chub Hurley pointed at the water pump near the ranch house.

"Take a shot at that cistern pump, Jeb," he said. "See if you kin put it out of commission."

Suddenly those at the fence heard a loud shout from the lower yard, near the bunkhouse.

"Hey, Hurley, you son of a bitch!"

Chub Hurley twisted his big frame in the saddle, looking for the source of the voice, He saw the stranger and the old man walking slowly towards him and his men. Jeb Frankel turned to his boss.

"It's the saddle bum, boss! And the old man!"

"Yeah, I kin see that," Hurley growled.

Frankel watched the two coming on for a moment, then shouted down at them, "Hey, old man, what the hell you doin' here? You workin' for her, now?"

"I just might be, Jeb," Nate said. "Oh, and I told her how we used to rustle her cows, too. Haw!"

"I'd call that squealin', you old son of a bitch!"

"Call it what you want, Jeb," the old man sneered. "I don't care one bit!"

"Well, I can't let that pass, old timer. Sorry, but I'm gonna have to put you down!"

"Then make yer move, mister, I ain't got all day."

"You've seen yer last sunrise, Nate Prescott!"

Jeb Frankel pulled his gun but never got off a shot. Old Nate Prescott's bullet hit him square between the eyes. Jeb's legs turned to mush and he fired a bullet into his own foot as he collapsed in a heap in the snow and died.

While the old man was concentrating on Jeb Frankel, Chub Hurley, quick as a snake, blindsided him with a snap shot, hitting him off center, just below his ribs. The old man grunted and sat down in the snow just as the stranger drew and fired. His bullet hit Chub Hurley in the chest with a loud thud.

The big Bar J ramrod glanced down at his chest then looked over at the stranger.

"Lucky shot. I had the drop on you, you sidewinder!"

Big Chub Hurley flipped backwards off his horse, into the snow. His horse, startled, walked backwards over his body, and ran off. Hurley never twitched a muscle.

By now, the stranger had his gun pointed at the remaining Bar J cowboys. "Who's next?"

They held their hands up, palms facing the yard "This ain't our fight," one said.

"Smart choice. You all know what to do, so get it done and go," the stranger said.

One of the cowboys rode out to get Chub Hurley's horse. He brought it back and they tied Hurley on it. They did the same with Jeb Frankel then headed back for Caldwell Springs.

A few moments later the Circle M cowhands came riding in from the west, kicking up snow. They thundered into the yard and quickly dismounted, crowding around the old man. Nate slowly put his gun back in its holster, smiling weakly.

Mrs. McCloud yelled from the porch. "Bring him up here, boys!" She ran into the house, got the medicine kit, and returned just as they were carrying the old man up the steps. "Put him on the chaise!" she said, pointing. They laid Nate on the chaise lounge.

"We heard shooting," Tim Gary said, "so we came back, thinking there was trouble. It looks like there was."

"Get his coat off, quick," Jan McCloud said. They got Nate's coat off and Jan pulled his shirt up around his chest. She then cut a long slit in his winter underwear, to expose the wound.

"What happened?" Henry Fuller asked.

"Five of Jarvis's men rode in," the stranger said. "Only three rode out." He was reloading his Colt.

"Who bought it?" one of the cowboys asked.

"Hurley and Frankel," old Nate managed to say, proudly. "Brazos and I, we took 'em both down. You shoulda seen us, right pard?"

The stranger nodded. "You still got it, old man. You still got it."

"Chub and Jeb? Man, I woulda like to have had a piece of that pie!" the kid said.

Jan cleaned the wound, studying it. "It went clean through, Nate." She went to work. In a few minutes she had a pad and a tight bandage on it to stop the bleeding.

"He needs a doctor," someone said.

"The hell I do!" Nate groaned. "I'm fine."

Jan closed the medicine kit. "Bring him along, boys." She went into the house and upstairs to one of the empty bedrooms. In a few minutes the stranger came in, helping the old man along. He laid Nate on the bed and went back down to the porch and rolled a cigarette.

"She's giving old Nate the royal treatment," young Fuller chuckled.

"He earned it," the stranger said.

There was a sudden solemn quietness. The stranger could sense, almost feel, the tension. Tim Gary looked down at his hands. He sighed and looked out into the yard.

"What's eating you, Tim," Henry Fuller asked. He, too, had gotten a whiff of it. It was pure fear.

"This ain't going to be good," Gary said.

"Jarvis?" the stranger asked.

"Yeah. After what you and the old man did, it ain't safe here anymore." He cleared his throat nervously. "Jarvis is gonna bring in the gunnies. He's gonna take the Circle M, sooner or later, and now, with this, there's no tellin' what he'll do."

The stranger shrugged, not knowing how to respond. Maybe it was true, maybe he and the old man did make things worse for Jan McCloud and her children. Jarvis would have to hit back. He had no choice. It was a matter of pride. He would hit back and hit hard.

"So, what do you think is going to happen?" Henry Fuller asked Tim Gary.

"He'll hire a bunch of saddle bums to burn down the line shack. Then he'll start picking us off, one at a time." Gary's voice stuck in his throat.

One of the other cowhands spoke up. "And you can bet the cattle will start to disappear, and finally the bank will foreclose on her. She might as well pack up and leave. Sell at a loss and get whatever she kin get…" His voice trailed off.

"How long you been here," the stranger asked Tim Gary.

"About ten years, I reckon." Gary said.

"Did you know her husband well?"

"Not very well. He was kind of a loner. She did most of the work, running the spread and all. She thinks Jarvis had him killed."

"What do you think?"

"I don't know. He gambled a lot. He did a lot of womanizing behind her back, if the rumors are true. Maybe a jealous husband or boyfriend did it. It could have been anybody."

It began to snow again. The cowboys went over to one side and began to whisper to one another.

"What's that all about?" the stranger asked.

"They're having a pow-wow," Gary said.

"About leaving?"

"Yeah. They won't risk bein' shot in the back."

"Will they go to work for Jarvis?"

"They might, but I doubt it. They'll most likely move on." Then, "Well, good luck, Brazos or whoever you are."

"What? You leaving, too?"

"I got a girl in town," Gary said. "I'll take her to Wichita and find a place where they ain't no war going on."

"What about your pay?"

"Pay?" Gary chuckled. "We ain't been paid for three months now. If it weren't for the food and care, there wouldn't be nobody here except the chickens."

"She's that broke?"

"She sure is," Gary replied and walked down into the yard and over to the bunkhouse. The others nodded to the stranger and followed the man who was once their boss.

The snow was falling steady, now. The stranger looked over at the bunkhouse for a moment then shrugged and went into the house. He found Jan in the kitchen drinking coffee. The twins came in from the living room and stared at him.

"Are you gonna leave, too," little Alice asked.

He smiled at her and mussed her hair. "Nope!" The twins ran off.

"I don't blame the boys," Jan McCloud said.

"You heard us talking."

"Yes."

"I'm sorry."

"For killing Chub Hurley and Jeb Frankel?" Jan asked. He nodded. "I would have done it myself, if I was a man." Then, "Jarvis will come after you for that. He'll pay somebody to do his dirty work."

"Yeah, I know."

"It's best that you move on, today. Now."

"No, I won't run. I'm in the middle now."

"If you stay here I'll be digging your grave up on the hill, next to my husband."

"What about you?"

"Me? I'm finished. I'm just waiting for the last hit."

The stranger studied Jan McCloud's face for a while. She looked away.

"Is there a place you can take the twins?"

Jan shook her head. "Yes, at the Flying B. My friend, Verna, is there with her husband Ed Brown."

"You should leave them there until we ride this thing out."

"Again, this isn't your problem, Mr. Brazos," Jan said. "There's no 'we' here to talk about. It's just me."

Suddenly they heard horses out by the corral fence, moving slowly towards the road. Moments later they rushed away at a full gallop. After that it was very quiet except for the ticking of the clock in the living room.

"They were fine boys," Jan McCloud said. "I'll miss every one of them."

There were footsteps on the front porch. Someone came up and knocked on the door. Jan and the stranger went to look. It was Henry Fuller.

"Mr. Fuller," Jan said. "I thought you'd gone with the others. Why are you still here? I can't pay you."

"Well, ma'am," Fuller said, "I guess I'm so partial to your apple rhubarb tarts I just couldn't leave. They're worth all the gold in the world to me, ma'am."

"Then you'd best come on in, Mr. Fuller, and have a piece."

Later, in the kitchen, Jan checked the young man's wounds. She nodded. "You're a fast healer, Mr. Fuller. They're coming along just fine."

Henry Fuller looked over at the stranger. "Actually, another reason I stuck around is to see Mr. Brazos here get his ears shot off by Jarvis's men." He chuckled.

"Where are you from kid?" the stranger asked.

"I'm from the Oklahoma Territory. By the Cimarron River. Why?"

"Well, from now on, you're the Cimarron Kid. Henry Fuller is gone."

Fuller chuckled again. "Yeah, I like that Brazos!"

6.

Bernice Jarvis sat in her wheel chair, and stared through the bedroom window on the second floor of the Bar J ranch house. The room was dark except for the light from the candelabra on the table by the bed, behind her. She watched the snow falling in the front yard and waited and waited.

It used to be a once a month waiting while Tern went to the Cattlemen's Association meeting with her never knowing what time he would come back. Then he came up with excuses to go into town more often. Once a month turned into once a week. Now he would go without so much as a single word of warning.

She could smell the scent of that other woman whenever he came home and fell drunk into bed beside her.

Once Bernice Jarvis had been a big part of his life, running the ranch house with flourish and flair, flaunting their wealth and station. Her handprint was on everything. She even supervised the cattle book accounts. She worked the servants tirelessly and kept everything moving. Everyone feared her.

She had parties and gatherings at the Bar J that were the envy of the town. Christmas was her favorite time of the year. Tern always lavished expensive gifts on her, diamonds, pearl necklaces, rings, and such.

Then, one day in spring, Tern gave her a beautiful mare for her birthday. From the very start Bernice and animal did not get on well together. Not at all. The mare had a mind of her own and that was just too much for the mistress of the Bar J Ranch. She would show the horse that she was boss by bending and breaking the animal's spirit. She had done that to many other horses in the past.

Bernice's favorite learning tool was the whip.

She set up a hurdle course and forced the mare to jump obstacles, raising them higher and higher. When the mare balked, she would whip it until it bled and cried for mercy like a human. No animal would get the best of Bernice Jarvis.

Then, one day, what was bound to happen did happen. The mare balked and Bernice went sailing aloft.

The stable boy watched in awe and inner delight as his mistress went soaring high in the air with a look of surprised horror on her face. There was a resounding crack as Bernice Jarvis landed some distance away on her back.

That was three years ago, and she never struck another animal again.

Bernice and Tern Jarvis had been good together in those early days. He truly loved her and treated her like a queen. She wanted for nothing.

They lived in Chicago where he managed her father's bank. When he learned about the lucrative cattle business to the west, and the opportunities to be had, he convinced his new bride that fate was calling them. This is where they could build an empire.

Then a friend told him about Caldwell Springs, the little cattle-shipping depot alongside the Santa Fe Railroad, out on the Kansas plains. There he could buy up small ranches for practically pennies on the dollar. The ranchers were mostly un-educated, ignorant, and naïve. It would be easy pickings, if you went there with plenty of money at your disposal. All you needed was money. Tern Jarvis had plenty of that, and he understood the power of it.

So they came and conquered Caldwell Springs. In five years Tern Jarvis had become the biggest rancher in the area. He hired only the best and hardest to run his empire, men who were loyal to the double eagle, as long as it kept coming, and never questioned his word. Those who weren't committed to the Bar J were cut and dumped.

He sent his profits to the bank in Chicago to be invested.

But those happy days were all gone now. After Bernice was confined to a wheel chair Tern seemed to submerge himself in the business of the ranch, especially the buying of more ranches. Once a month he would take a train east to Chicago to check on the bank. He would stay for a week or more before returning, but never sent her a wire to keep in touch.

She silently watched this change in her husband, and gave up expecting him to administer to her deep need for companionship. She was lonely and felt isolated and he didn't seem to notice. She had tried to strike up a friendship with people like Chub Hurley and Jeb Frankel, people she detested for their crudeness, but they kept their distance. She hated all of them as she watched them leap upon their horses and ride like the wind while she rotted in a wheel chair.

These were the thoughts that ran through the mind of Bernice Jarvis as she sat in her bedroom staring out of the window at the falling snow, waiting for her husband to return from town drunk and smelling like a whore.

She started to cry.

7.

Old Nate Prescott was the first to hear them. He groaned and crawled out of bed, holding his side as he struggled to look out the window. From the upper floor he had a clear view of the road from Caldwell Springs. Jarvis's fancy English buckboard and a single rider were coming straight for the yard.

"We got company," the old man yelled to those downstairs in the kitchen.

Jan McCloud, Henry Fuller, and the stranger had just finished breakfast and were discussing her situation. She got up and went through the living room to the door to the porch. She took one look and yelled back into the kitchen.

"It's him and Marshal Sledge!"

She heard the twins coming down from their bedrooms, into the kitchen. She put that in the back of her mind as she watched Jarvis's man drive his fancy rig up into the yard and stop several yards from the porch. Rolly Sneed, the bank man who served eviction notices, sat beside Jarvis. They were both bundled up in fur coats, and wore wool scarfs to keep out the cold.

Marshal Sledge also came into the yard. He stopped near the rig and yelled with authority, "Widow McCloud! Come out here!"

Jan came outside, onto the porch, and stood there staring down at Jarvis's rig. Jarvis avoided her eyes as the bank man climbed out with a white paper in his hand. He stopped at the porch steps and handed it up to Jan McCloud. She took it and folded it, but didn't look at it. She knew it was an eviction notice.

"I'm sorry, Mrs. McCloud. It's my job."

"I ain't blaming you, Mr. Sneed," she said. "But why is the Marshal here? Jarvis afraid I'll bite him?"

"I had nothing to do with that," Sneed said. Then he said in a quavering voice, "Ah, ma'am, Mr. Jarvis now owns the Circle M. He bought up your debt to the bank. I'm sorry."

The bank man paused a moment then reached into his coat pocket for another piece of paper. He held it out to her.

"What's this?" she asked.

The bank man sighed. He looked uncomfortable.

"It's a check for seven-hundred dollars. It's from Mr. Jarvis for your equity in the Circle M. He wanted to be fair."

"I bet!" Jan McCloud glared over at Jarvis.

"Please take it, ma'am," the bank man said.

"Don't touch it!" a voice said. The stranger came out onto the porch, wearing his gun. He looked at Jan McCloud. "I'll take that." He took the check from the bank man and the notice from Jan, and tore them into small pieces and tossed them away. The pieces were caught up by the wind and scattered. Rolly Sneed stepped back, both intimidated and uncertain. He was, by nature, a gentle man.

The Marshal dismounted and swaggered over to the porch. He was a tall, thin, gaunt man with a wind-burned face. He stared up and down at the stranger with black, dull eyes then slowly pulled his sheepskin jacket back to expose a pearl-handled Remington forty-four. The stranger, hatless and without his coat, stood staring back at the Marshal. For a moment it looked as if they were going to draw on one another.

Suddenly the stranger smiled. "Good-morning, Marshal. It's been a long time."

The Marshal was suddenly taken aback. He stared hard at the man before him, squinting. "Have we met, stranger?"

"Yep!"

"When…where?"

"You've got a short recollection, Marshal," the stranger said. "It was Cheneyville?"

The Marshal seemed to be concentrating hard. He started shaking his head no, when a look of awareness came over his face.

"You! What the hell are you doing here!" the Marshal growled.

"What am I doing here? Well, I'll tell you, Marshal, I'm doin' whatever I feel like doin'. If you have any objections, let's hear it now."

The stranger stepped down into the snow, walking straight at the Marshal. The Marshal backed out of the way. He watched the stranger go over to Jarvis's rig.

"You Jarvis?" the stranger asked.

"Yes, sir, what can I do for you mister?"

The stranger stared in at Tern Jarvis, smiling.

"Are you one of them slick businessmen from Chicago, Mr. Jarvis?"

"Yes, I'm originally from there. Why do you ask?"

"You came here and bought up all the small ranches and made your mark out here, did you?"

Tern Jarvis remained silent. He'd seen these kinds before. Ignorant saddle tramps who didn't know when to shut up, with an inflated feeling of self-importance.

Jarvis suddenly struck out with the riding crop he always kept in the rig as a status symbol. The stranger caught his wrist and yanked. Jarvis tumbled out, face down in the snow.

Just as the Marshal went for his gun Henry Fuller came out on the porch with his Colt drawn.

"I wouldn't try that, Marshal!" the kid said calmly.

The Marshal froze. He pulled his coat over his gun and backed off a few paces and watched as Tern Jarvis got up on his feet and brushed the snow off his coat. He picked his hat up and got slowly back into his rig. He stared at the stranger and smiled.

"I don't know who you are or where you came from, mister, but you should leave here as soon as you can. Your life might be in danger." Jarvis's voice was cold and very menacing, but it was what he didn't say that was chilling.

The stranger recognized him as a man who would strike like a rattlesnake but without the warning, and he would go for the kill, letting others do the dirty work.

Jarvis nodded as the bank man got in the rig with him. In a moment his driver had it heading out onto the road to town. The Marshal got back on his horse. He stared at the stranger.

"You've just took on more than you can handle, my friend," Marshal Sledge said. "You should ride on." He turned his horse out of the yard and raced to catch the ongoing rig that was now far in the distance.

Back in the kitchen the stranger, Henry Fuller and Jan McCloud watched Nate making breakfast for the twins.

"What was all that talkin' about out there, mom?" Alex asked.

"Nothing important, honey, Jan replied. Then, "Say, it looks like Uncle Nate has cooked you guys up some flapjacks and eggs. Isn't he nice?" Alex only nodded and kept shoveling food into his mouth.

Jan sat down and watched the twins eat for a moment then said, "How would you both like to spend a few days over at Aunt Verna's house and get to play with Tobey and Nell?"

"Oh, yes, could we?" Alice cried happily. Alex nodded yes.

"Good, we'll go over there right after breakfast, then."

Jan McCloud took the stranger and Henry Fuller aside. "I'm taking them over to the Flying B. They can't stay here."

"I'll go with you," the stranger said.

An hour later the twins were bundled up in the back of the buckboard. The stranger sat next to Jan as she steered the horse from the yard and onto the road. They headed east towards Caldwell Springs, but quickly turned north at a crossroad.

"Why was Marshal Sledge afraid of you, mister?" Jan asked.

"Was he?"

Jan stared hard at the stranger for a moment, a puzzled look on her face. He knew she was studying him but looked straight ahead.

"Yes, he seemed very afraid."

"I hadn't noticed."

"Who are you?" That's all Jan could think of saying. She repeated, "Who are you, mister?"

"They call me Brazos."

Jan shrugged. "But that's not your real name, is it?"

"No."

"How come the Marshal knows you?"

"I was a bounty hunter once, years ago. When things got slack I gambled on the side, just to keep the money coming in. I met the Marshal briefly once at a poker game in Cheneyville. That's how he knows me."

Jan let that ride a moment, and then said, "So, why are you taking up my fight, Mr. Brazos?"

"I don't know, ma'am, it seems like the right thing to do."

"You don't have a death wish, do you, Mr. Brazos?"

The stranger chuckled. "Not that I'm aware of, ma'am." He paused a moment. "What about you? All you had to do was take that seven-hundred dollars and go someplace and start over with the twins and stay alive."

"When you have roots, you can't do that," Jan said. "His parents and my parents are buried up on a hill behind the ranch house on the Circle M. To me that's sacred ground. I can't let Jarvis walk all up and down on it. Not while I have a breath left in my body, I won't. Can you understand that, Mr. Brazos?"

Without hesitation, the stranger said, "I can and I do, ma'am."

They didn't talk much after that exchange. Jan looked back to check on the twins. They laying side-by-side on a pile of burlap bags wrapped in a blanket. In an hour they were at her brother-in-law's small spread called, the Flying B.

The twins ran upstairs to join Tobey and Nell. Jan introduced the stranger to Ed Brown as a new hand.

"There's a storm a brewin'," Ed Brown said, as he stood by the fireplace packing his pipe. "I kin feel it in my bones, Jan. And it doesn't concern the weather."

"You mean Jarvis?"

"Yeah," Ed said. "He's been steppin' on too many toes lately. He's grabbin' too much too fast. People are wonderin' just what he's up to."

"I've seen his kind before," the stranger said. "They get a hold on a place and squeeze the breath out of it. They take it all and leave nothing for anyone else."

"That's Jarvis," Verna said angrily.

Ed nodded. "The sad thing is, someday Jarvis will look like small potatoes. It'll get worse. All we'll have is the here and the now of it. Small spreads like ours will be gone, like dust in the wind."

"How long did Jarvis give you?" Verna asked Jan.

"He wants me out now," Jan sighed.

Ed Brown lit his pipe and blew a cloud of smoke. "It just ain't right. There's gotta be a way to stop that carpetbagger."

"I don't see how, with the bank and the law on his side," Jan said.

"You can't stop him now," the stranger said. "It's too late. He's got almost the whole valley under his brand. The rest of you will have to sell, eventually."

"Some people say it's progress, but I say it's it legal stealin'," Ed Brown said. "You work your ranch until you're dead and it ends up bein' sold off to some land grabber by the bank!

They ate dinner and Jan got ready to leave. She hugged and kissed the twins, and then her sister in law.

"Thanks, Verna," she said. "You, too, Ed. Thanks for taking the twins."

"Don't worry about them, Jan. They'll be just fine. You do what you have to do and come back safe," Verna said. She turned to the stranger. "You'll watch out for her, won't you Mr. Brazos?"

"I'll try," the stranger said.

They left. The snow was falling hard and the going was slow. It was late evening when they finally got back to the Circle M. They felt exhausted, drained of emotion. There was now only her, old Nate, young Henry Fuller, and the stranger left.

And she knew something bad was coming her way.

8.

There was a weed-grown graveyard on the north side of Caldwell Springs where they buried vagrants and drunks. Tern Jarvis had the bodies of Chub Hurley and Jeb Frankel buried there. He quickly forgot their names and who they were. They represented failure and had no part in his book of success.

After the degrading event at the Circle M, Tern Jarvis was in a vengeful mood. He brooded for a day then met with Marshal Sledge in his office at the jailhouse.

"I want him out of the way permanently," Jarvis said. "Who is he, anyway? Some gunny trying to get in tight with the McCloud woman?"

"I don't know where he came from, but I know who he is," the Marshal said. "It all came to me again, when he mentioned Cheneyville."

"What's that all about? Cheneyville?" Jarvis asked. He pulled out a cigar and lit it. The Marshall suddenly seemed deep in recollecting long lost memories.

"It was about five years ago. Old man Petrie was the Marshal then, and I was his Deputy. There was a poker game going on over at the Pink Pig Saloon. We heard a shot and knew right away there had been a contention over cards."

"Go on."

"Well, old Petrie and me heard it and knew somethin' was up so we hustled over there. We went in and saw Jack Cordell standing over Red Hardy. Hardy was dead as a mackerel. One bullet dead center in the heart."

"Who was Red Hardy?"

"At the time, he was considered the fastest draw in the territory. He killed over thirty men, all fair and square," Marshal Sledge said. He chuckled. "I think Hardy was glad he was done for."

"Why is that?"

"Well, having a reputation as a fast gun does have its drawbacks. Young bucks came along once a week, wantin' to brace Hardy and take his title, wantin' to be known as the kid who outdrew the famous Red Hardy." The Marshal chuckled.

"And now it was this Cordell."

"Yeah, it was him, alright. And by the look on his face, he knew what he was in for."

"What happened?"

"Well, the word spread fast as a prairie fire. Jack Cordell was now the man to beat. And they came like flies to honey. The very next day Cordell shot it out on the streets of Cheneyville no less than three times before nightfall. There was betting going on about who would kill him."

"My God! What savages!" Jarvis said, with a scornful laugh. "It must have been fun to watch. Like a circus."

"Yeah, but the next day it was all over. Petrie ordered Cordell to leave town, and he left."

"Where did he go?"

"No one knows. He just fell off the map."

"Until now."

The Marshal nodded. "Yeah, until now."

"He's probably been on the run all those years. He's probably not as fast on the draw as he used to be."

"Unless he keeps in practice, most of them do."

"Is there anyone around these days who can beat him?"

"There is one. Rand Carter."

"Who's Rand Carter?"

"He hires on to whoever offers the most. He used to be a bounty hunter. One day he was hired by a Cattlemen's Association, in Texas, to solve their rustling problem. Carter hunted them down and killed all twelve of them."

Jarvis whistled. He was very impressed. "My God! I love that man! Can you contact him?"

"I could send a wire to the Marshal in Fort Worth. He's married to Carter's sister. He could probably get word to him." Then, "What's your limit?"

"He can name his own price." Jarvis was excited. "Just get him here, Marshal, and your re-election is assured."

The Marshal chuckled. "That should be somethin' ta see. Jack Cordell going up against Rand Carter."

"And that will solve our problem with the Circle M," Jarvis mused.

He drew on his cigar and blew a cloud of scented smoke over at the Marshal.

9.

"Are you sure you want to do this, ma'am?" the stranger asked Jan.

"Yes, but you don't have to stay, mister." Jan left it unfinished. She suddenly realized she didn't know his real name.

"Brazos is just fine," the stranger said.

Jan McCloud liked this unassuming man. He was quiet but deadly. She liked the quiet part. It calmed her down.

"Have you ever been in love, Mr. Brazos?"

He was caught by surprise with the question. It had nothing to do with the current dire situation. He wondered why she asked it.

The stranger chuckled. "I came close once. It was a schoolteacher."

"What happened there?"

"She married the principal. I was only ten."

"Very smart of her." They all laughed.

"No, I've never settle down long enough to get involved, ma'am," the stranger said.

They were sitting in the kitchen with old Nate and young Fuller. Nate and the kid were playing poker for matchsticks.

"Do you believe in a God, Mr. Brazos?" Another of her surprise questions.

"Sometimes, yes. Sometimes, no. I try to, but it can be hard."

"That's how I feel, too. Sometimes you get the feeling God might have fallen asleep on the job."

Old Nate chuckled. "Yeah, I've had that feelin' fer a long time, now. Haw!"

"Well, there ain't nobody I know of who died and came back to tell," young Fuller said. "Anyway, it's how you live and die what's important."

"How's that?" Nate asked.

"Well, if you lead a good life and help people who are in need, then God ain't got no bone to pick with you, does he?"

"I guess that lets me an' Brazos out, then," chuckled old Nate. "We're the biggest sinners there is. We kilt people, didn't we Brazos?"

"Well, I wouldn't brag about it if I was you," Fuller said. "That's when God will smite you down!"

Fuller looked over at the stranger. "How do you think you'll buy it, Brazos? Fair and square?"

"I hope so," the stranger said.

"How sad," Jan said.

Nate chuckled. "He'd be better of ifen you shot him, ma'am. Dyin' by the hand of a purdy gal is the best way to go! Haw!" They all laughed.

"Mr. Prescott. You do amaze me," Jan said. "That was very romantic, coming from you." They laughed some more then let the silence in.

Finally Henry Fuller said, "They'll be comin' tomorrow to force you off your land, ma'am."

"Yes. I know, Henry."

"Would you call me Cimarron, ma'am? I really hate bein' called Henry."

"Of course, Cimarron."

"Thank you," the young man said. "It's like in one of those stories I heard about where they hit you on the head with a sword and say, "Get up, you scury Knight!""

"Very eloquent," Jan McCord said. "Yes, you are indeed my knight in shining armor, Sir Cimarron."

"If I meet a gal, I'll tell her my name is Cimarron. She'll most likely swoon over thet."

"I'm sure she will," Jan said. "I'm certain of it."

The stranger looked over to one corner of the kitchen where six lever-action Winchesters leaned against the wall. He went over and picked two up by the barrel, and took them into the living room and put them on the table there. The kid brought in two and left just as Jan McCloud brought in the last two. There were boxes of shells already on the table.

Jan went to the window and looked out. There was nothing to see except the blanket of snow glistening in the yard in the moonlight. None was falling, and it was quiet and still outside. A rabbit came out of somewhere and stopped by the fence to sniff around. They watched until it darted off out of sight. It left tiny footprints in the snow.

"Please go, and take the old man with you," Jan said calmly. "I don't want any more killing."

"I can't. Anyway, he won't go. He wants to put things right with you. He feels he owes you something. And he's right, he does."

"But you don't. There's no cause for you to stay."

"Yes there is. It's the code," the stranger said. "Some men, like old Nate, are born to the code. Men like Jarvis don't recognize the code. I'm going to shove it down his throat, make him choke on it."

She understood. It was the code of the west, born hundreds of years ago in the days of chivalry. The code to protect helpless women and children from evil men like Jarvis. It would never die. It might waver and wane, but it would never die out completely It only took one spark to keep it alive.

The stranger turned to face Jan. She looked at him. He saw what her eyes were saying. She nodded. He tilted her chin up and bent to kiss her. He held it a while until he felt her shudder and sigh, then he held her in his arms.

"I'll die protecting you," he said.

"God bless you," she whispered.

"And you."

They walked back into the kitchen. It was late. Jan banked the fire in the kitchen stove and put out the lights. They went upstairs to sleep.

In the morning, at the breakfast table, they heard horses out front. They all went out onto the porch to look. Three of Ed Brown's Flying B cowboys dismounted.

"Mr. Brown said you were in dire straits, ma'am," one of the cowboys said. "He asked for volunteers. Here we are. I think there's more a comin', ma'am."

"Kin we use yer bunkhouse, ma'am?" another said.

"Go home, boys, please," Jan McCloud pleaded.

They ignored her and led their horses down to the bunkhouse. Just as they went in another bunch of riders came crashing into the yard from the Box N spread. Others kept coming off and on. By evening the bunkhouse had twenty cowboys in it.

A lookout spy, stationed in the nearby aspens by Jarvis, saw it all. By evening he was reporting back to Jarvis.

10.

Hiring killers to kill other killers was going out of vogue. It was getting to be seen as a waste of resources to pay bounty hunters to do the job that a sheriff and a posse were paid to do. Let the law take care of the lawbreakers. People like Rand Carter were not so much in demand any more.

When Carter got the message from Marshal Sledge, who lived in a one horse town called Caldwell Springs, Kansas, telling him to name his price, he hurried to get himself and his horse on the next train in that direction.

Rand Carter got off the train on a Thursday afternoon, got his horse, and trotted through the deep snow over to the Marshal's office. He tied it to the rail and went in. Tern Jarvis was smoking a cigar while talking to Marshal Sledge when Carter walked in on them.

Carter was a very thin, gangly, square-jawed man, of average height. He had a tight-skinned, skeletal face with eyes set far back in his forehead, eyes that blazed out at everything in sight under his wide-brimmed hat. He had a flat nose with flared nostrils that gave out a wheezing sound when he inhaled and exhaled. A long mustache over his upper lip covered most of his mouth.

But the strangest thing about Rand Carter was his arms and hands. The arms seemed to be too long for his body and his hands, inside the kidskin gloves, were enormous.

"Hi, Marshal," Carter said in a soft, almost whispering voice. He didn't offer to shake hands. He looked at Tern Jarvis. "You the man I'm working for?"

"Welcome to Caldwell Springs, Mr. Carter. I've heard so much about you." Then, "If you need or want anything, just ask and it is yours, sir."

"Thanks, I will," Carter said dryly, not impressed.

"I understand there is a fee," Jarvis said. "Do you require that up front or after the job is done, Mr. Carter?"

Instead of answering, Rand Carter sniffed the air and smiled. "You don't happen to have one more of those fancy cigars, do you?"

"It so happens I do, Mr. Carter," Jarvis said.

Tern Jarvis got another Havana Bravura from his gold cigar case and gave it to Carter. He looked at it, smelled it, and then bit a chunk off on end and started chewing it. He put the rest in his sheepskin coat pocket.

"Have a seat, Carter," the Marshal said, pointing to a chair next to Jarvis and himself.

Carter sat down and stared at Jarvis as he chewed and wiped tobacco juice off his bony chin. For some reason, he grinned, as if to say, "That's what I think of your damn cigar!"

Jarvis cleared his throat. "Marshal Sledge, perhaps you would bring Mr. Carter here up to date on the situation?"

"Sure," the Marshal replied. "You see, Rand ---"

"Mr. Carter!"

"What?"

"I'll let you know when to call me Rand, Marshal," Carter said with a broad smile. He seemed to be toying with them both. They chuckled nervously.

"Oh, sure," the Marshal replied, trying to hide his feelings. He had just been chastised by Carter and didn't like it. "Well, we have a situation out at the Circle M spread. Mr.

Jarvis just bought it and the previous owner refuses to leave, and ---"

"It's my job to see they leave, dead or alive?"

The Marshal nodded. "Something like that."

"I don't see the problem here, Marshal. You're the law, ain't ya'?"

"The problem is they've got maybe twenty, thirty armed cowboys out there, led by a gunslinger called Jack Cordell. Ever hear of him?"

"Yeah. He outdrew Red Hardy, years ago. So he's out there, huh?" Carter chuckled. "That's real nice. I like that."

"Why do you like that, Mr. Carter?" Tern Jarvis asked.

Carter ignored the question again. "It's been a long trip and my horse and I are a mite weary, gentlemen. What I'd like right now to start with, is a hot bath and a half raw one pound steak smothered in onions with potatoes and green beans and some beer to wash it down with."

"And you shall have it, sir," Tern Jarvis said. He stared at this enigmatic person for a moment and asked, "So, just how fast are you Mr. Carter?"

Carter stood up and went towards the door and turned to face the two men. "Blink."

Jarvis stood up. "What?"

"Blink, just once."

"Alright, sir." Jarvis said. He blinked once and when he opened his eyes he was staring at the barrel of Rand Carter's Colt. The man had drawn with lightning speed. Jarvis caught his breath. "My God! You are fast!"

"I used to be a lot faster," Carter said. "I'm getting old now. All these bullets I'm carrying around in me have slowed me down some." He holstered his gun. He coughed and cleared his throat. There was something odd about the man. He seemed to belong to a by-gone era, a remnant of the past. There was also a hint of sadness there.

An hour later Rand Carter was ensconced in the most expensive room the Majestic Hotel had to offer. He dined on steak, potatoes, green beans, and beer. After that, Tern Jarvis took him over to the Cattlemen's Association Building for champagne, and oysters. This time Carter smoked a cigar instead of eating it.

By midnight he was totally drunk so Jarvis had him carried over to his room. The Marshal and he went back to the Marshal's office.

"A very strange man," Jarvis said.

"Yeah, but fast as lightning," the Marshal replied. "And that's all that counts. Tomorrow Jack Cordell will be dead and widow McCloud will be out of your hair. The Circle M will be the Bar J."

"Very good, Marshal. And just to be sure there are no complications I'll have my Bar J cowboys with me. You have Mr. Carter ready to go."

The Marshall held back a moment then said, "What if Cordell gets lucky?"

"Then the Bar J boys will finish the job."

They shook hands and parted company. Tern Jarvis felt very good.

Early in the morning the Marshal and Jarvis met at the jail.

"We got a problem," Marshal Sledge said. "Carter wants ten thousand up front."

Jarvis gave that some thought. "Alright, I'll get it from the bank. After this is finished we'll figure a way of getting it back."

"How?"

"We'll get him drunk again. When he passes out you'll rob him or kill him or both."

"That won't be easy."

"I'll have some of my men help you. You can deputize them."

"Alright, then, I'll take care of it," the Marshal said.

"Good, now let's go do what we have to do. I want the Circle M in my hands by noontime."

"And you'll get it. I promise," the Marshal said.

11.

A day after they arrived to fight for the Circle M, some of the cowboys began to have second thoughts. The rumor that the Marshal and Jarvis had a small army of fifty men cooled their hot heads somewhat, and they started riding one-by-one back to their spreads. It was cold and the weather was nasty. Counting the stranger, Nate, and Fuller, that made a total of nine. Nine to face thirty or forty.

Jan McCloud and young Fuller went down to the bunkhouse to talk to those who were left.

"Boys," she said, "I appreciate what you're all doing for me, but I'd rather you went back to your spreads. This is only going to end one way, anyhow. You'll be dead and I'll be driven off my land. That's how it will end. I don't want your deaths on my conscience, so please do me a favor, and go home."

One of the cowboys spoke up. "If Jarvis pulls this off, my spread might be next, ma'am. We gotta stop that carpetbagger here and today!"

Another yelled, "We're gonna make a stand here that people will remember for years to come, Mrs. McCloud! Come hell or high water, we're gonna kick Jarvis's ass all the way back to Chicago!"

There was a strong sense of bravado in the air and Jan McCloud could feel it and the tight bonds that cowboys felt. They started patting each other on the back and vowing to stand and fight. A few let out loud rebel yells and Indian warpath screams.

Suddenly the clamor died down as the distant sound of pounding horses got louder and nearer. They stood motionless, listening uncertainly. The moment of truth was approaching with a vengeance.

Henry Fuller poked his head through the open bunkhouse door. "You gotta see this, boys," he said, with a chuckle. "My-oh-my! We're really in for it!"

Everyone rushed to look up to the yard.

Forty of Jarvis's Bar J cowboys were lined up along the fence facing the Circle M ranch house. Jarvis's fancy rig was next to the open gate. He sat alone, staring at the porch. The snow-packed yard was empty. The Marshal was next to the rig. His horse danced nervously, sensing the tension.

Suddenly the Marshal shouted out, "Jack Cordell! Come out here! Someone wants to meet you!"

Everyone stared at the ranch house door, waiting for it to open.

"Come on out, Jack, and meet your maker!" the Marshal screamed. The cowboys at the fence watched and waited.

Finally the front door opened slowly and the stranger stepped out onto the porch. He was hatless and wore no coat. The wind snapped at his shirt and rustled his shoulder length black hair. He took a visual survey of the fence and sort of sneered as he walked casually down into the yard.

The Marshal turned in his saddle and looked back to where Rand Carter was on his horse. "Go earn your money, Carter!"

The Marshal nudged his horse aside to let Carter through. Carter dismounted at the gate and walked slowly, with measured steps, into the yard. He stopped twenty feet from the stranger.

Rand Carter stared at the stranger for a short moment. "So, you're what all the fuss is about?"

The stranger nodded. "Looks like it."

"That asshole gave me ten grand to kill you," Carter said. "It's right here in my shirt pocket. When I'm finished with you, I'm goin' back to town and get me a whore."

The stranger remained calm and silent. He shrugged as if to say he didn't really care. Rand Carter looked over at Jarvis where he sat huddled in his fancy rig.

"I hate sons a bitches like him," Carter said, "but I gotta make a livin', don't I?' The stranger showed no emotion, no interest. He kept standing there in a disinterested way.

It started to snow again, very hard, and seemed to get colder. The wind picked up.

Rand Carter suddenly turned nasty. "Where do you want me to put it, Cordell? I kin put it between yer eyes or in yer heart. Any special spot you want it?" The stranger gave him a half-smile. "No? Then maybe I'll put it in your belly. It hurts more there." He got no response. "Yer a dead man Cordell and I'm finished talkin' to you. You smart-assed son of a bitch!"

Rand Carter drew with lightning speed, but somehow he couldn't finish the draw. His hand stopped moving and he fired into the ground. He felt a numbness in his heart and felt a hot wetness spreading inside his shirt, moving slowly down his chest. The fire in his eyes had gone out. He watched dully as the stranger reloaded his Colt and put it back in its holster.

"Thank you," Carter gasped. "Take my horse and rig. It's yours." His body seemed to shrink in on itself as he went down on his knees, dropping his gun in the snow.

The stranger rushed to him, catching him in his arms as he collapsed. He gently lowered him to the ground, holding him.

"Take the money, Cordell, you won the pot," Rand Carter muttered. His breath rattled in his chest. It was very quiet in the yard. A large, black crow landed on the bunkhouse roof and cawed loudly, then flew across the yard, over to Jarvis's rig. It stopped on top to defecate, then flew off.

Jarvis pointed at the stranger and screamed, "Kill him! Kill them all!"

The stranger heard the click of gun hammers being pulled back. He looked up into the barrels of death.

"Hold it, men!" Old Nate came limping out on the porch, holding his side. He stopped to hang onto the porch railing.

"Men," old Nate yelled, "most of you know me, rustled cattle with me, and got pissy-assed drunk with me! And we fought rustlers together, too, and wild fires and floods! We rode different brands at times. But we never went against the code, did we?"

The old cowboy stopped to catch his breath.

"You're decent men and you know it. Jarvis, here, wants you to do indecent things. But if you're a real cowboy, you won't! You'll abide by and honor the code, and the code says to protect women and children! We're all brothers in the code, men, but not Jarvis. He don't believe in the code. He don't follow the code." Nate stopped a moment. "And that's all I got to say, you sons a bitches!"

Nate held on to the porch rail for support. He looked pale and tired and worn. Jan rushed up on the porch to hold him.

There was a strange silence, and then there was the sound of guns going back into holsters. Horses were turned and went pounding down the road towards Caldwell Springs. Finally there was only Jarvis and the Marshal.

"Go get my money back, Marshal," Jarvis growled.

The stranger was still down on his knees holding Rand Carter when the Marshal drew without warning. His horse shied a bit at the sudden move and his shot missed its target but hit Carter in the side. Suddenly a shot came from the direction of the bunkhouse.

The Marshal swung sideways in his saddle. His horse bolted off, dragging him by one leg down the road. His arms flailed wildly in the snow. The stranger looked across the yard to see Henry Fuller reloading his smoking Colt.

"Thanks, Cimarron," the stranger said loudly. The Cimarron kid smiled.

Jarvis's driver turned his rig around and went fast towards town. He was in shock.

The stranger took the roll of money out of Rand Carter's pocket just as Carter's horse came over to nuzzle his body. Suddenly it smelled the blood and went running away into the nearby field.

Young Fuller came up and asked, "Should I go get it?"

"No, it'll come back when it gets hungry."

Fuller stood looking down at Carter's body as the stranger walked up on the porch to Nate and Mrs. McCloud.

The six remaining cowboys mounted up and left for their spreads. It was all over.

Jan, Fuller, and the stranger took old Nate into the house and set him down by the kitchen stove to warm him up. Jan made a fresh pot of coffee and they sat at the table to drink.

"How much is the balance on your mortgage?"

"Two thousand, why?"

The stranger took the roll of money out of his pocket and handed it to Jan. She stared at it.

"What's this?" she asked.

"It's the pot. Ten thousand," he said. "I won it from Carter, fair and square. The horse and rig, too. Here. Take it."

"I can't take this. I'm sorry, it's blood money."

"You can take it. Think of your sacred ground on the hill, the twins, and all the sweat you put into the Circle M. Are you going to let Jarvis take it all away from you?"

"I can't!"

"Then, Jarvis has won. Is that what we fought for?"

Nate said, "Take it, ma'am." Henry Fuller nodded.

Jan stared at the stranger for a moment, then sighed and took the money roll.

The stranger and young Fuller went out into the yard and carried Rand Carter's body into the barn and wrapped it in a horse blanket. They planned to bury him up on the hill, when the snow stopped.

12.

There was something about the title, Cattle Baron that gripped Tern Jarvis. To him it sounded like royalty. The terms banker and rancher didn't, somehow, have the same lofty resonance. He read the investment news about the surging prices of cattle and how men such as Chisum, White, King, and Goodnight had made their fortunes in the cattle business. It was still wide open and thriving.

Tern Jarvis aspired to enter this thrilling new world that he read about in books, and in the news.

Moving from Chicago to Kansas meant leaving the bank, and tearing Bernice away from her high social life and the Equine Social Club where she was top rider on her jumping team of the obstacle course. Riding had always been her one and only passion. It gave her a high social standing, which was further enhanced by her efforts to save the lives of injured horses, injuries caused by people like herself.

When Tern made the decision to move out west without discussing the matter with her, she felt left out, of course, but remained silent to please him. She played the role of the good, obedient wife.

At first Tern made several trips to Caldwell Springs without her. His first acquisition was the small Flying B Ranch. It had only two-thousand head of cattle but ample water. The owner, a drunk and a gambler, was four payments behind on his mortgage. Jarvis bought him out. It was so easy it surprised him. These were simple people of the land, gullible, easily influenced, and no match for him.

In a few months he and Bernice made their move out west. They planned to have a family, but her accident put that aside. Jarvis fell into his work with a passion and kept his mind on his goal of owning all the ranches in Caldwell Springs Valley. It would not be hard to do since the bank was lax, and the ranch owners where negligent in their payments.

One-by-one, Tern Jarvis cut deal after deal. His empire began to grow and he soon became a person of notice. His name began to echo throughout the valley as a force to be reckoned with. He supported the Cattlemen's Association as a lead member, and practically had Marshal Sledge elected by a landslide.

What he failed to recognize was that he was an outsider, and no amount of money could make him one of them. He had no roots, no inner connection to the land.

Also, Jarvis was ignorant of their ways, of the way they thought and lived, something ingrained in their souls by fighting for the land and bleeding for it in years past. They and the land were as one. If you pulled their roots from the land, they would die. And Jarvis was doing just that.

Jarvis really didn't care about the land or the people. He was sure that sooner or later he would own every ranch in the valley. He would be a Cattle Baron. No one could stop him.

No one except the widow McCloud. She had done what no one else had been able to do. A few moments ago, outside Caldwell Springs, on a cold, snowy day, she stopped him in his tracks.

As his rig raced back towards town, Tern Jarvis sat rigid with hate and anger. He would crush that flea of a woman. This wasn't the end of him, but it would be the end of her. He legally owned the Circle M, and if it took a court order backed by an army of lawyers and lawmen, she would be uprooted and tossed out.

Jarvis thought about the ten-thousand dollars he had left behind, now probably in her hands. Seth Porter, at the bank, might just let her get away with paying her debt off, so he would have to talk to Seth about that. It might be hard because the McCloud family were old stock here.

And the Marshal? He had proved worthless in this whole affair. A bad investment. Jarvis would get rid of him in the next election.

In half an hour Jarvis's rig was sitting in front of the Cattlemen's Association Building, and he was walking up the stairs to the bar while his driver sat in the lobby dozing off. Jarvis lit a Havana Bravura and ordered a rye and bitters on the rocks.

Jarvis looked around the big, well-lit room. It was full. Suddenly he realized that everyone had stopped talking and was looking in his direction. He nodded and held his glass up, but no one did the same. It was as if he was an intruder, and they wondered where he came from and what he was doing there.

He turned back to the bar and finished his drink. He wanted to order another but the waiter had gone off into the back of the bar. All of a sudden he felt very alone. There was no one at the bar with him. No one was near him.

Suddenly he heard it. It started low, a muted pounding sound that slowly grew in volume. The floor began to shake beneath his feet and he wondered if it wasn't perhaps the start of an earthquake. But no one was running.

He turned to look and saw its source, its cause. All the ranchers were stomping the floor with the heel of one boot. The force and the sound of it hit him hard like a blow from an iron fist.

The great Tern Jarvis was being drummed out of the Cattlemen's Association!

For a moment Jarvis was frightened, but only for a moment. He put his drink down on the bar, crushed his cigar out in the ashtray, stiffened, and turned around to face the crowd.

"You can go to hell, all of you!" Jarvis screamed like a wounded animal.

He then walked slowly, proudly, and confidently downstairs. His driver followed him outside. In a few minutes his rig was across town and parked in front of the Majestic Hotel.

He went up to his private room and waited. Soon she came.

13.

Bernice Jarvis sat in her wheelchair looking out of her bedroom window at the snow falling in the yard two stories below. She was tired. Not physically tired just tired of life, her life.

For all practical purposes her life was over and she had no future, only memories of a life that now seemed like a beautiful dream. It had been a good happy life up until the accident, and she had memories of it to hold on to. But they had faded further into the past, and grown dimmer. They just weren't enough to sustain her or hold her up anymore.

As for Tern, he was a stranger shutting her completely out of his life. He spent more time in town than he did at home. They hardly exchanged words anymore. As a substitute for conversation, he gave her books to read, the latest novels brought in on the mail train from Chicago.

Bernice Jarvis knew about the woman and the room at the Majestic Hotel. In a small town like Caldwell Springs it wasn't hard to find things out if you had resources such as money and servants who had friends at the hotel. She knew a lot about Tern and what the town and ranchers really thought about him. She often confronted him about that very subject.

"You think you're one of them, now, don't you," she smirked. "Big Cattle Baron! Well, you're a fool for thinking that, my dear. They hate you and they're laughing at you! And you're too stupid to see it!"

"I have no idea what you're talking about, my love," Tern Jarvis said. "And neither do you!"

"Oh, yes I do," she said sarcastically. "If you knew what they thought about you, what they say behind your back, you would sell everything and go back to banking in Chicago."

"Rubbish!"

"And speaking of banking, my dear husband, you never did love me, did you? It was all about my father's bank, wasn't it? You knew I'd get it after he died, didn't you?"

"I did love you and I do love you, Bernice."

"I don't believe you. You're not the same man I married ten years ago. You're a complete stranger."

"I...I'm trying to build a future for us, my dear, and that takes up much of my time. Eventually things will smooth themselves out and we'll spend more time together."

But that turned out to be a lie. He had taken a mistress in town, and she was just in the way. She lost him for good to some painted tart in Caldwell Springs. But she didn't blame that women. She cursed Tern for being such a weak man and she hated him for it.

Suddenly she heard the rig coming into the yard. It stopped a moment to let Tern out, then went on over to the barn. Wheeling herself over to the fireplace she looked up at the clock on the mantel. It was four in the morning. Tern would come up, take off his coat and jacket, and fall asleep drunk on the bed. He wouldn't say a word or look at her.

Bernice Jarvis maneuvered her wheelchair over to the end table by the head of the bed. She pulled open the drawer, took out a key, and put it in her nightgown pocket. Then she wheeled herself slowly over to a far corner, into the shadows, out of sight, and waited, staring at the small candelabra on the table some distance away. She kept staring at it as if hypnotized, like a moth fascinated by a flame.

She sat and waited.

She sighed a sigh of relief when she heard her husband's loud footsteps on the stairs. Seconds later he opened the bedroom door and lurched into the room on unsteady legs, tearing off his coat and then his jacket as he entered. He was muttering incoherently under his breath as he headed straight for the bed. He collapsed down near the edge, one of his arms hanging limp, his hand touching the floor rug.

"You can all go to hell," he muttered, then fell silent.

Bernice Jarvis stayed in the shadows watching her husband, listening to his deep, raspy breathing. After every three or four breaths he would whine and snort like a pig. This is how it always went. She had been listening to his sickening sounds for years. It would, as usual, go on all night. She dared not lay beside him because he would, with no warning, flail about like a fish, hitting her with his elbow or fists, as he fought some demon in his nightmare dreams.

Bernice started to cry knowing Tern would not awake to her sobbing, to ask what was wrong. He wouldn't come to soothe her or hold her. Those days were over.

She wheeled herself over to the bedroom door. After carefully closing and locking it, she tossed the key into the fireplace. Next she got the candelabra from the table.

She stared at the candle flames for a while then slowly wheeled herself over to the four-poster bed. Tears ran down her cheeks as she looked at her husband. She moaned as if in pain, shaking her head from side to side as if fighting an inner struggle.

She sighed. Her struggle was over.

She was very calm as she set fire to the bed blanket and curtains on her husband's side of the bed, careful not to disturb him. She wheeled herself around to the other side and rolled out of the wheelchair onto the mattress. She tossed the candelabra down by her feet and then turned on her side to embrace Tern Jarvis in a tight grip.

"I love you, darling," she sobbed. "Let's go home."

The flames began to spread.

14.

It was springtime and the wisteria on the side of the ranch house was in full bloom. The yard was full of newborn chickens and hens getting under foot. Six-month old foals pranced about the barn and corral.

The Circle M Ranch had a crusty old ramrod named Nate Prescott, also known by many as Cheyenne. His sidekick was a young buck with a scar on his left ear and temple. His name was Henry Fuller and he was known by many as the Cimarron Kid. Rustlers far and wide steered clear of the Circle M because of these two gunslingers.

The Jarvis's had no will because there was no one to receive anything. With no children, the bank took over the Bar J holdings and broke it down into the original ranches. The cattle was divided according to their last cattle book tallies, and the previous owners were given a chance to get back what Jarvis had taken from them. It all worked out fine.

The ranchers ended up with a lot more cattle than they had when Jarvis bought them out. That was because Nate knew the secret location where Chub Hurley and Jeb Frankel hid the stolen cattle, cattle that had grown in numbers for years while waiting to be sold behind Jarvis's back. So it all worked out pretty well. The Circle M ended up with almost ten thousand head of cattle. The market was favorable.

"Ma'am," Nate vowed, "this time next year, the Circle M will be drownin' in beeves. You mark my word. Cows will be comin' out our ears!"

Jan McCloud had her ranch back and money in the bank as well. She hired cowboys that were screened by Nate and Fuller. In a year she expected to turn a profit. With the grass looking good and plenty of water, there was no reason why she couldn't.

Then there was the stranger, also known as Brazos.

He stayed in the background helping when he could or was asked to. Fuller and the old man were practically inseparable. Brazos worked as hard as the rest and asked for no special treatment. He didn't press himself upon Jan, even knowing she wouldn't, most likely, reject him. He didn't want her to think she was in his debt.

But Jan McCloud knew this man was not the ranching type. He proved that with his gun. The signs were that he was restive and ready to move on. He never told her that he was a gunfighter who had to keep moving to stay alive. She wouldn't, couldn't be tied to a man like that.

One day, when the men came back from the range, he wasn't with them. Nate and Fuller wore sad faces. She knew that the stranger had kept going and would never come her way again.

She would never forget him.

The End

About the Author

R. Annan is a seasoned and traveled author with many interests. As a career serviceman he served in Korea and Vietnam. He also completed a one-year course at the Defense Language Institute at Monterey, California, and graduated from the University of South Florida with a B.A. in Art and Art History. After taking a two-year course in screenwriting at the Hollywood Scriptwriting Institute, he established *The Old Time Radio Club Time Machine* as both a scriptwriter and an actor.

A Note from the Author

Thank you for reading my book. If you enjoyed it, would you please consider rating and reviewing it? I'd enjoy your feedback. Here is a link to my author's page on Amazon: www.amazon.com/author/rannan

Look for other books to appear soon. Thank you!